# The Twelve Days of CHRISTMAS DOGS

written and illustrated by Carolyn Conahan

DUTTON CHILDREN'S BOOKS

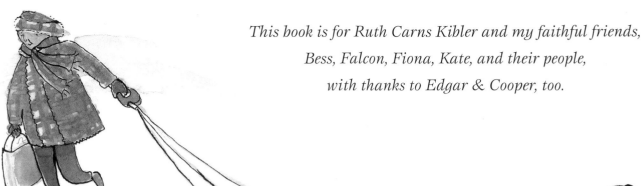

*This book is for Ruth Carns Kibler and my faithful friends,*
*Bess, Falcon, Fiona, Kate, and their people,*
*with thanks to Edgar & Cooper, too.*

DUTTON CHILDREN'S BOOKS
*A division of Penguin Young Readers Group*

Published by the Penguin Group
Penguin Group (USA) Inc., 375 Hudson Street, New York, New York 10014, U.S.A. • Penguin Group
(Canada), 10 Alcorn Avenue, Toronto, Ontario, Canada M4V 3B2 (a division of Pearson Penguin Canada Inc.) •
Penguin Books Ltd, 80 Strand, London WC2R 0RL, England • Penguin Ireland, 25 St Stephen's Green, Dublin 2, Ireland
(a division of Penguin Books Ltd) • Penguin Group (Australia), 250 Camberwell Road, Camberwell, Victoria 3124, Australia
(a division of Pearson Australia Group Pty Ltd) • Penguin Books India Pvt Ltd, 11 Community Centre, Panchsheel Park,
New Delhi—110 017, India • Penguin Group (NZ), Cnr Airborne and Rosedale Roads, Albany, Auckland 1310, New Zealand
(a division of Pearson New Zealand Ltd) • Penguin Books (South Africa) (Pty) Ltd, 24 Sturdee Avenue, Rosebank, Johannesburg 2196,
South Africa • Penguin Books Ltd, Registered Offices: 80 Strand, London WC2R 0RL, England

Copyright © 2005 by Carolyn Conahan
All rights reserved.

Library of Congress Cataloging-in-Publication Data

Conahan, Carolyn.
The twelve days of Christmas dogs/by Carolyn Conahan.—1st ed.
p. cm.
Summary: In this variation on the folk song "The Twelve Days of Christmas," children exchange gifts
of various types of dogs, from "a pug puppy under the tree" to "twelve doggies drumming."
ISBN 0-525-47486-2
1. Children's songs—United States. 2. Christmas music—Texts. [1. Dogs—Songs and music. 2. Christmas—
Songs and music. 3. Christmas music. 4. Songs.] I. Title.
PZ8.3.C738Tw 2005
782.42'1723'0268—dc22 2004028814

Published in the United States by Dutton Children's Books,
a division of Penguin Young Readers Group
345 Hudson Street, New York, New York 10014
www.penguin.com/youngreaders

Manufactured in China • First Edition
1 3 5 7 9 10 8 6 4 2

*O*n the first day of Christmas, my best friend gave to me...

*a pug puppy under the tree.*

On the second day of Christmas, my best friend gave to me...

*two turtle dogs*

*and a pug puppy under the tree.*

## three French dogs,

*two turtle dogs,*
*and a pug puppy under the tree.*

On the fourth day of Christmas, my best friend gave to me...

*four collie dogs,*

*three French dogs, two turtle dogs,*
*and a pug puppy under the tree.*

On the fifth day of Christmas, my best friend gave to me...

*five golden dogs,*

*four collie dogs, three French dogs, two turtle dogs,*
*and a pug puppy under the tree.*

six pooches playing,

*five golden dogs, four collie dogs, three French dogs, two turtle dogs, and a pug puppy under the tree.*

On the seventh day of Christmas, my best friend gave to me…

*seven splashy swimmers,*

*six pooches playing, five golden dogs, four collie dogs,*
*three French dogs, two turtle dogs,*
*and a pug puppy under the tree.*

*eight pups—all milky,*

*seven splashy swimmers, six pooches playing, five golden dogs,*
*four collie dogs, three French dogs, two turtle dogs,*
*and a pug puppy under the tree.*

nine doggies dancing,

*eight pups—all milky, seven splashy swimmers, six pooches playing,*
*five golden dogs, four collie dogs, three French dogs, two turtle dogs,*
*and a pug puppy under the tree.*

On the tenth day of Christmas, my best friend gave to me...

ten Labs a-leaping,

*nine doggies dancing, eight pups—all milky, seven splashy swimmers,*
*six pooches playing, five golden dogs, four collie dogs,*
*three French dogs, two turtle dogs,*
*and a pug puppy under the tree.*

*eleven yapping yippers,*

*ten Labs a-leaping, nine doggies dancing, eight pups—all milky,*
*seven splashy swimmers, six pooches playing, five golden dogs,*
*four collie dogs, three French dogs, two turtle dogs,*
*and a pug puppy under the tree.*

On the twelfth day of Christmas, my best friend gave to me…

*twelve doggies drumming,*

*eleven yapping yippers, ten Labs a-leaping, nine doggies dancing, eight pups—*
*all milky, seven splashy swimmers, six pooches playing, five golden dogs,*
*four collie dogs, three French dogs, two turtle dogs,*
*and a pug puppy under the tree.*